THAT WON'T DO YOU NO GOOD! IF HE WANTS YOU, HE'LL TAKE YOU.

WHO...? WHO WILL?

THE REAPER. MONSIEUR DEATH!

TWEEEE

THOOM BRAKATATATAT PTINGPI

MGOD! ⚡ **GROAN** ⚡ **OWWWOOoH!** **GOD! HELP ME!** **EEEE-YAHH... OH**

A CASUALTY REPORT! TAKE THIS BACK WITH YOU, CORPORAL!

H-HOW MANY, SIR?

TOO MANY!

SIX HUNDRED DEAD! THE COUNT WILL GO HIGHER.

HELP ME! OH, GOD! HELP ME...

WELCOME TO VERDUN, CORPORAL!

CORPORAL! COME BACK HERE!

YOU CAN'T HELP!

BRATA TATATATATAT. AT. TA

PTHUNK THUNK

ZA PLUN

DAMNED! WHAT A WASTE!..

FTOOM

...A SENSELESS WASTE!

2ND ARMY HEADQUARTERS, SOUILLY

MAJOR MARAT HAD ASSIGNED ME THE MISSION. I TURNED OVER THE CASUALTY LIST.

AS I HEARD IT, GENERAL NIVELLE WAS BUSY TELLING JOKES WHEN THE REPORT ARRIVED.

HMM. GET DOWNSTAIRS AND CLEAN UP FOR SUPPER. WELL DONE, CORPORAL.

NIVELLE—WHO HAD ORDERED THE BLOODY AND USELESS ATTACK.

ELLE, WHO ONLY HOURS
LIER WAS CELEBRATING...

THE NEW COMMANDER
THE 2ND ARMY.
NG OVERDUE,
ROBERT!

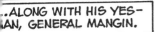

..ALONG WITH HIS YES-
AN, GENERAL MANGIN.

HE WAS REPLACING
PETAIN, WHO WAS
PROMOTED TO
SECTOR COMMANDER.

ATTACK FORT DOUAUMONT?
TO WHAT PURPOSE?

PURPOSE?

THE MEN WILL BE
RUSHING MACHINE
GUNS AND ARTILLERY
FIRE — *UPHILL!*

I SHOULD *HOPE* YOU
HAVE A PURPOSE
IN MIND.

SIRS. GENERAL
JOFFRE.

AT EASE,
GENTLEMEN!
I HAVEN'T MUCH
TIME. I'M
EXPECTED AT
THE BALLET.

POLITICIANS,
YOU UNDERSTAND.

NOW, GENERAL,
I UNDERSTAND YOU
HAVE AN OPERATION
IN MIND...?

I DO. AN
IMMEDIATE
ATTACK... *HERE!*

AN ATTACK ON DOUAUMONT?
EXCELLENT. I WILL AWAIT
THE RESULTS.

WHAT?!

FORT DOUAUMONT

CHAN
MEUSE

VERDUN

YOU *CAN'T*
AUTHORIZE
THIS!

I JUST
DID!

JUST LIKE *THAT?!* WHAT IS
THE ENEMY STRENGTH?
HOW MANY GUNS? HOW MANY
MEN? IT IS *EASY* TO ORDER
AN ATTACK FROM THE
COMFORT OF THIS ROOM...

SENSITIVE? SOLDIERS SHOULD BE MADE OF STERNER STUFF. I'M SORRY IF I GAVE OFFENSE, GENTLEMEN! *AU REVOIR.*

HOLD ON...

...WHY ARE YOU TELLING *ME* ALL THIS? I'M VERY BUSY.

YES, I KNOW...

...WE'VE BEEN OVER THAT, MR. "PIRATE-OF-WALL-STREET."

THE TERM IS "ACQUISITION SPECIALIST."

DON'T INTERRUPT *ME*, YOUNG MAN!

YES, YOU'VE "ACQUIRED" THIS AIRLINE WE'RE O IT'S LOSING MONEY. SO *YOU'RE* GOING TO MAKE IT PAY BY *SELLING IT OFF* — PLANE BY PLANE!

YES. SO..?

WITH NO REGARD FOR THE PEOPLE WORKING FOR YOU — THE PILOT, THAT CUTE STEWARDESS? WHAT ABOUT THEIR JOBS?

I'M NOT IN THE EMPLOYMENT BUSINESS. MY FIGURES...

FIGURES? WE'RE TALKING ABOUT HUMAN *LIVES!* I SAID BEFORE YOU REMIND ME OF SOMEONE. NOW SIT BACK AND LISTEN! I HAVE A *POINT* TO MAKE.

I TOLD YOU HOW I ENLISTED WITH REMY? YES, YES. WELL, NOW YOU KNOW HOW I GOT THE PHONY NAME AND THE BELGIAN UNIFORM.

MY AND I HAD BEEN SPLIT UP INTO FERENT OUTFITS, BUT I DID MEET AGAIN. AT A FRENCH MILITARY PITAL IN VERDUN.

AAAGH! OWW-OHH! TAKE IT OUT!

ORDERLIES. QUICKLY!

STOP IT! YOU'RE DELIRIOUS!

THEY DIDN'T GET IT OUT! OHHH...!

NO—I CAN FEEL T! THEY MUST OPERATE AGAIN! OH, THE PAIN..!

RESTRAIN HIM. TIE HIM DOWN!

MAKE THEM STOP— PLEASE!

HE'S A DANGER TO HIMSELF!

I'M A FRIEND. I CAN CALM HIM.

VERY WELL.

HOW ARE YOU, REMY?

COULD BE BETTER, MON AMI.

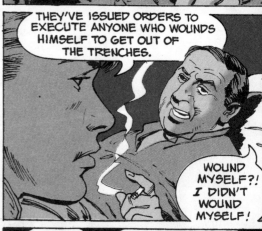

HA! VERTIG! FINISHED!

...WAS WAITING TO PICK UP AN ORDER FOR ...TILLERY SHELLS WHEN I MET HIM... ...E GUNNERY SERGEANT.

OH, MY MARIE! MY BEAUTIFUL MARIE!

YOU ARE SO BEE-OO-TIFUL, CHERIE!

AHH—ENJOYING YOUR RUBDOWN, EH?

...THINK I BLUSHED—LIKE I'D WALKED IN ...AN INTIMATE LOVE SCENE. BUT SGT. ...MILLE WAS DELIGHTED. HE'D FOUND ...AUDIENCE TO SHARE HIS LOVE WITH!

...SHE'S YOUR BASIC ...05 MILLIMETER. PRETTY ...ITTLE PIECE O' DESTRUCTIVE MACHINERY.

LITTLE?

ONLY THROWS A 35-POUND SHELL! NOT LIKE THIS BABY!

IT'S HUGE!

YOU CALL THAT HUGE?

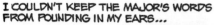
I COULDN'T KEEP THE MAJOR'S WORDS FROM POUNDING IN MY EARS...

THE GERMANS DON'T TAKE SPIES *ALIVE!*

VOICES. A BAD SIGN. HAD TO GET HOLD OF MYSELF.

HELP ME! HELP ME!

?!

NOW THE MOANS OF THE DEAD...?

NO — SOMEONE *IS* OUT HERE!

I'M...SHOT IN THE LEGS...AND STOMACH. I...CAN'T...WALK.

HOW LONG HAVE YOU BEEN HERE?

SINCE YESTERDAY.

I HAD A VISITOR, BUT I TOOK CARE OF HIM.

I'LL GET YOU OUT, SOLDIER!

DON'T LEAVE ME!

I'LL BE BACK. I PROMISE!

CORPORAL...?

M-MAJOR GASTON?

QUICKLY NOW!

PONG

PTING

FTHUD

THE GERMANS ARE BRINGING UP ARTILLERY?

I DON'T NEED A *SPY* TO TELL ME *THAT!*

BATTALION HEADQUARTERS

LISTEN TO HIM, COLONEL.

AND YOU'D BETTER HAVE A SEAT!

THEY'RE BRINGING IN TWO BIG BERTHAS!

WHAT?!

THERE'S SOAP, WATER, AND A COT IN THERE! WE GO TO 2ND ARMY HEADQUARTERS AT DAWN!

MAJOR MARAT! STAY A MOMENT.

SIR?

I BELIEVE NEW ORDERS ARE CALLED FOR!

FOR WHAT?

TO CALL OFF THE ATTACK, OF COURSE!

YOU *ARE* GOING TO CANCEL THE ATTACK, ROBERT?

IN THE NAME OF GOD!

WE'VE ALREADY BEGUN THE BOMBARDMENT!

CALL IT OFF!

YOU DON'T UNDERSTAND, PHILIPPE—

I'VE BEEN *ORDERED* TO ATTACK!

ROBERT, IF YOU LET THIS ATTACK PROCEED, KNOWING WHAT YOU KNOW...

YOU ARE COMMITTING COLD-BLOODED *MURDER!*

VERY WELL! YOU DO IT, THEN.

YOU CALL OFF THE ATTACK.

MAJOR— GET THIS TO THE FRONT!

YES, *SIR!*

WHO'S THAT?

JOFFRE! THE COMMANDER-IN-CHIEF!

AH, NIVELLE! MANGIN!

-!- HRMPH -!- PETAIN.

GREETINGS, GENERAL JOFFRE. HOW HAVE YOU BEEN?

I'LL BE MUCH BETTER WHEN WE RETAKE FORT DOUAUMONT.

WHAT'S THAT? SOUNDS LIKE THE BOMBARDMENT HAS STOPPED!

ROBERT! IT SOUNDS LIKE THE SHELLING HAS STOPPED!

YES...IT HAS, SIR!

?!

IT'S NOT TIME FOR THE ATTACK YET.

NO, SIR...

THEN WHY AREN'T THE GUNS FIRING? THE ATTACK MUST BE SUPPORTED BY ARTILLERY!

YES, I UNDERSTAND THAT.

GENERAL JOFFRE, THE GUNS HAVE STOPPED FIRING BECAUSE I *ORDERED* THEM TO STOP!

YOU DID *WHAT ?!*

I ALSO *CANCELLED* THE ATTACK!

NIVELLE, DID YOU *AGREE* TO THIS?

I—I—WELL, YES...

NO EXCUSES, NIVELLE!

I ORDERED AN ATTACK! I *WANT* AN ATTACK!

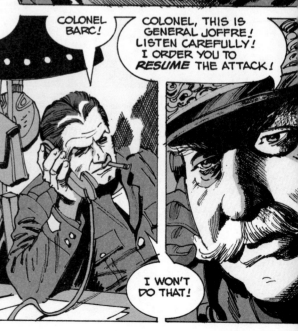

COLONEL BARC!

COLONEL, THIS IS GENERAL JOFFRE! LISTEN CAREFULLY! I ORDER YOU TO *RESUME* THE ATTACK!

I WON'T DO THAT!

WHAT?! I WON'T DO THAT BECAUSE I *CAN'T* DO THAT!

COLONEL, THIS IS THE COMMANDER-IN-*CHIEF* OF THE FRENCH ARMY!

I AM GIVING YOU A *DIRECT ORDER!*

AND I AM LOOKING AT AN ORDER CANCELLING THE ATTACK--

--SIGNED BY GENERAL PETAIN. A WRITTEN ORDER CAN ONLY BE CHANGED BY *ANOTHER* WRITTEN ORDER!

IF YOU *ARE* GENERAL JOFFRE, YOU WILL UNDERSTAND...

...BECAUSE *YOU* WROTE THAT REGULATION!

THOOM
THOOM
THOOM

NOBODY EVER FOUND OUT WHAT I DID.

THE FRENCH FINALLY DID RETAKE FORT DOUAUMONT. NIVELLE WAS A NATIONAL HERO AND, FOR A WHILE, COMMANDED THE WHOLE FRENCH ARMY.

FINIS